ARTIVERSE PUBLICATION
PRESENTS

The Unwaning Moon of Desires

Compiler
Sundhar

ARTIVERSEPUBLICATION

Title: **The Unwaning Moon of Desires**

Compiler: **Sundhar**
Co Compiler – **Poorna Krishnaa KJ**

Language: **English**
Manuscript By: **Artiverse**
Edited By: **Artiverse**

ISBN - **978-81-997856-7-0**
Price: **299/-**

Distributed By: **Amazon, Kindle, Flipkart, Google Play Book, Meesho and offline bookstores**

Published by **ARTIVERSE PUBLICATION**
Prakhar Agrawal
MIG – 83, Bandhavgarh Colony, Satna, Madhya Pradesh, Pin Code - 485005

Email id: **artiverse81@gmail.com**
Mobile no: **9179591620**

ACKNOWLEDGEMENT

This anthology was not written in isolation, though much of it was born in solitude. The Unwaning Moon of Desires owes its existence to the quiet forces that sustained the writing when words felt distant and to the unseen constellations of people, moments, and memories that shaped its emotional gravity. I extend my deepest gratitude to time itself—for its patience, its pauses, and its refusal to rush healing or clarity. I also take this opportunity to thank my parents, my fellow co-authors and my dear friends for all the support they have provided me with. Many of these poems were written in hours when the world slept, and for that stillness, I am thankful. Silence has been both a companion and a teacher. My sincere appreciation goes to those who believed in the necessity of expression, even when it arrived fractured, raw, or unresolved. To the voices that listened without judgment, and to the absences that taught me what longing truly means—both have left their indelible mark on these pages. I am grateful to literature, poetry, and language for their enduring mercy: for allowing pain to become metaphor, desire to become rhythm, and memory to become something survivable. Every line in this collection stands on the shoulders of the poets and thinkers who taught me that words can ache, and still illuminate. Finally, this work is for the reader—known or unknown—who has ever looked at the night sky and felt that certain desires do not wane, but quietly endure. If these poems find you at the right moment, then the journey of writing them has been complete.

DISCLAIMER

This anthology is a work of fiction. The publisher has made every effort to carefully edit and curate the contributions of the co-authors and ensure that the content is free from plagiarism. All the write-ups included in this book represent the unique creativity and perspectives of the respective authors.

The compiler and editor have made their best efforts to review, edit, and present the content in an error-free manner. However, the opinions, ideas, and expressions in each piece belong solely to the respective co-authors.

Each co-author is entirely responsible for their own work and confirms that their content is free from plagiarism, libel, breach of privacy, or misrepresentation of facts. The compiler, editor, and **Artiverse Publications** shall not be held responsible for any such issues.

In case of any dispute, including claims of plagiarism or copyright infringement, the respective co-author will be solely accountable and may be subject to legal action.

ABOUT THE BOOK

Beneath the eternal gaze of the moon, human hearts rise and fall like tides, each pulled by a gravity of yearning that never wanes. The Unwaning Moon of Desires is an anthology that gathers voices from the edges of passion, solitude, and dream. Within these pages, poets and storytellers trace the shimmering paths of desire in all its forms, romantic, divine, destructive, and redemptive. Every tale and poem reflects a fragment of the moon's light: sometimes gentle and wistful, sometimes sharp enough to wound. From whispered confessions under starlit skies to the aching silence of love left unsaid, the collection explores how longing can both illuminate and consume the soul. For every desire deserves to be heard. Unheard desires manifest into dreams and nightmares that shape our actions one day. This book is a place for my fellow poets and writers to express their unheard questions, thoughts and expectations have buried deep down into their hearts. Let the moon guide you through these stories and verses, a celestial companion to the desires that refuse to die, and the hearts that refuse to stop reaching.

ABOUT THE FOUNDER

Behind Artiverse Publication stands a visionary with a heart for art and a soul for stories. Dev Agrawal, coming from Sangam city Prayagraj, this young founder, is a passionate writer, curator, and dreamer who believes in the power of words to create change. With a mission to give voices to budding authors, poets, and creators, he built Artiverse as a haven where creativity meets opportunity. From handwritten drafts to published works, he's dedicated to nurturing talent, amplifying unheard voices, and celebrating art in every form. His journey isn't just about building a publication—it's about weaving a vibrant universe of storytellers who inspire, empower, and connect.

IG - **words.bydev**
Call - **9179591620**
Mail – **devkumar120803@gmail.com**

Table of Contents

Compiler

Sundhar

A singer, songwriter and a bard.

Strangers With Memories

Like the tides of the night, That reach for the moon's hand,
Memories of us play in unison like a band, But everything dissipates once I realize it, Like the waves had hit the land,
The breeze that was once of nostalgia, Is now slapping me on my face, Saying that I'm a disgrace,
And that it was me who ruined it all, And that I'm supposed to take on the fall, It's rolling my head round like a ball,
I still yearn for those now-greyed memories, To live through them all over again,
Much like the tides of the night,
That reach for the moon's hand without fail, I still yearn for all those people,
I still long for all those moments, Much like the moon and this blue earth, We've fragmented into strangers,
Now every passing look from them, Push me to the edge with pain,
And when we pass through like a couple of strangers, A part of me is yanked away...

Co-Compiler

Poorna Krishnaa K J

An Engineering Graduate by education and Digital marketing executive by profession. Started writing short stories and poems as a hobby and somehow got much more involved in the recent times. The songs and stories mostly deal with the past and delusions.

Still breathing…

Troubling silence in thin air, I can barely breathe in it.
Perception distance is a mile long, And I'm trying to decrease it.
As the times ticking, and my body's aching I don't know how's the other side doing As the times ticking, and my feet's moving
I am not sure what the hell I am doing.
I'm not sure if I'm content now...
But I am climbing anyhow.
Troubled silence in thin air, And I'm getting choked in it.
Expectations are sky high,
And I'm trying my best to climb it.
As the sun is setting, and my mind's thinking I don't know if the other side thinks of me As the time's ticking, and mind's dreaming I don't know what the hell I am doing.
I'm not sure if I'm content now...
But I keep climbing anyhow.

I’m chasing a fading star, away from the silence. I'm chasing a fading star, with too tired heels.
I'm chasing a fading star, away from the nonsense. I'm chasing a fading star, to see the other ones.

I’m not sure if I’m content now, But I keep falling somehow. I'm not sure if I'm content now, But I keep climbing anyhow.
Troubled silence in thin air,
Still, I’m breathing, I’m still here, breathing.

Shraddha Padhi

I'm a student from Odisha. Poetry has been my helping hand for expressing myself as I'm not good with words. But, I never thought I'd become a co-author someday. Beyond grateful for this opportunity and the whole team. By God's grace, thank you very much.

A past to remember

I might pretend everything is okay
But not having you by my side shatters my heart Without you this world is just blue and grey You were not just a friend but my counterpart
I miss every second of those eyes twitching You never admit what those eyes actually said Silent motions in our skin overflowing
You looked so mine when you laid

Catching your glimpse my heart rushes for a war Fine were those strands of hair when you fixed them Sometimes I just wanted to lock you in a jar
These sad-romantic songs made me firm
Now, all these are just stories narrated by my brain The way you defended me when I couldn't stand for myself
How I wanna dance once again with you in the rain Stays just a longing wish for myself
How your smile lit up my day
When I saw you crying for the first time my heart ached as if it's the last Can I describe what happened after that?
I may
I tear up as I remember my past

My eyes yearn for your presence

But my heart is bound by an everlasting pledge Times when I got hurt by your words or absence I guarantee I won't take revenge
Stay happy wherever you are Work hard whenever you have to Eat healthy and take care
Stop roaming to and fro.

Hemanya Kakkar

Born and based from Delhi. I'm an aspiring and passionate author that is dedicated to crafting poetries, poems and stories. With the passion of creating several genres like fiction,non-fiction, romance, mystery, etc to inspire people and to help them guide and create something fascinating. Through my writing, I hope to take readers to new places and stir up strong feelings. Welcome to my world of poetry, stories and some interesting genres. I did take part in many competitions online and did get my writing selected for a few books too

Loving You in Silence: A Letter to the One I Let Go

Dear Love,

I don't know if I should be writing this. Maybe it's selfish. Maybe it's unnecessary. Maybe it won't even matter to you. But my heart has carried these words for too long, and I need to let them go, just like I let you go.
It's been a while since we last spoke. A while since I last saw you, since I last held your hand, since I last called you mine. And in all this time, I've never stopped wondering,are you okay? Are you happy? Is life treating you well?
These are the questions I've held inside, but I've never had the courage to ask. I've typed your name into my phone more times than I can count, my fingers hovering over the keyboard, forming words that never got sent. Because what right do I have to ask? What place do I have in your life now?
You once told me you loved me. You held me close and made me feel like I was enough, even when I believed I wasn't. You saw something in me that I never could. But love, as strong as it was, couldn't silence the voices in my head. My insecurities, my overthinking, my fears,they built walls between us, walls I couldn't tear down, no matter how much I wanted to. So I did the only thing I thought I could. I walked away.

I told myself it was for the best, that I was saving you

from me. That you deserved someone who wouldn't question your love, someone who wouldn't doubt themselves every second of the day. Someone who wouldn't ruin something so beautiful with their own insecurities. And yet, even as I let you go, my heart never did.

I wish I could tell you how many nights I've spent lying awake, thinking about you. About us. About all the what-ifs that will forever remain unanswered. I wonder if you ever think about me too. Not in a longing way, not in a way that disrupts your happiness, but just in passing, like a song you used to love that plays on the radio unexpectedly. Do I ever cross your mind, even for a fleeting second?

I know you've moved on. I've seen the way you smile now, the way you look at her. And it hurts. It hurts in a way I can't put into words, but it's a pain I accept. Because if anyone deserves happiness, it's you. And if you've found that with her, then that's all that matters.

I won't lie and say I don't wish things were different. That I don't wish I had been stronger, more secure, more capable of accepting love without questioning it. That I don't wish I could turn back time and hold onto you instead of pushing you away. But wishing won't change anything. And loving

you still, after all this time, won't bring you back.

So, instead, I will love you from afar. I will love you in silence, in the spaces between my thoughts, in the quiet moments where your memory lingers. I will love you in the lessons you taught me, in the ways you made me better, even when I didn’t see it. I will love you in the way I hope for your happiness, even if it’s not with me.

Maybe one day, I’ll stop missing you. Maybe one day, I’ll wake up and you won’t be the first thing on my mind. Maybe one day, I’ll find someone who loves me the way I never let you. But for now, I carry you with me, in every unspoken word, in every unsent message, in every heartbeat that still whispers your name.

And if you ever wonder, just once, if I’m okay, know that I am. Or at least, I will be. Because loving you, even from a distance, has been one of the most beautiful things I’ve ever known.

Be happy with the one, you love. Be loved. And know that a part of me will always love you, even if it’s only in silence. I hope you know I long for you even when I shouldn't but i won't come between your happiness. Take care

Yours,
Ex sweetheart.

Kanishetty Lakshmi Harika

Kanisetty Lakshmi Harika is a passionate writer from Nellore, whose storytelling weaves together emotions, suspense, and depth. She has a keen interest in genres like crime, thriller, and love, crafting narratives that leave a lasting impact on readers.

Her journey as a writer began in 8th standard, initially as a hobby, but soon evolved into an unwavering passion. Over the years, she has honed her craft, bringing powerful stories to life with intricate plots and compelling characters.

With a natural flair for storytelling, Harika continues to create immersive experiences for readers, blending raw emotions with unforgettable moments.

ENDURING PROMISES

Deepa sat alone on the beach, clutching a letter in her hands. The rhythmic waves crashing against the shore mirrored the tide of emotions within her. As she gazed at the vast ocean, memories of her past swept over her, pulling her back in time.

I am Deepa, the only child of a loving family. A guitarist at heart, but also a final-year Computer Science student. Playing the guitar has always been my passion, a melody that defines my soul. Love, to me, is something special, meant for one and lasting a lifetime.

Then came Hari. A decent-looking guy with a playful, flirtatious nature. He was the type to be single yet act like he was ready to mingle. He often chatted with multiple girls in class, and I knew from the start that he wasn't someone to be taken seriously.

One day, I was late to class and was asking the girl next to me about the lecture when Hari, instead of her, answered my question. Though I hadn't asked him, he took the opportunity to speak to me. I found it strange but acted normal. Over time, he continued engaging in conversations with me, and soon, we became good friends. I knew his flirtatious nature, so I never took him seriously. But for Hari, things were different. When he was with me, he wasn't his usual self. He felt something deeper, something unfamiliar.

One day, he asked me, "Have you ever met your one?" I laughed and replied, "My one? LOL. No, I never have. You know me well." Hari hesitated before saying, "What if I told you that I'm in love with you?"

I was taken aback. "Are you serious? This isn't some prank, right?" He shook his head. "No. The day I met you, I intended to flirt, but as time passed, I couldn't think about anyone else. Being with you feels like an addiction for my heart."

I was speechless. I rejected his confession, but we continued being friends. At least, for me, we were just friends. But for him, things had changed forever. He chose to remain by my side, fearing he might lose me completely if he pushed too hard.

Days passed, and suddenly, he had to leave for another state for work. Before leaving, he asked me to meet him one last time before his week-long trip. I agreed, sensing something different in our dynamic. We had lunch together, and as I watched him walk away, I felt a strange emptiness. It was as if he

wasn't just leaving for a week, he was leaving a part of me behind. That night, he called. "Did you reach home?" I replied softly, "Yes."

Sensing my sadness, he asked, "Should I come back? Just say yes, and I'll be there in a few hours." I wanted to say yes, but I couldn't let him abandon his responsibilities for me. "No," I whispered. He assumed it was a rejection, but he never lost hope. He kept trying.

Time flew by, and we graduated. I never gave him an

answer, as it was a life- altering decision. I was cautious, afraid of making the wrong choice. Unlike this generation, where relationships are easily forgotten, I believed love was sacred, meant for one and only one.

At our farewell, I thought he would say goodbye. Instead, he said, "Deepa, I need to tell you something. When I saw you playing the guitar on stage, I imagined our life together. I don't want to say goodbye because I can't. I will never leave you. Just hold my hand once, and I will be yours forever. Wait for mc, and I promise I will return."

I hesitated. "I will wait as long as I have hope. But remember, if I lose hope, I won't wait anymore."

Hari smiled. "That's enough for me. I don't want you to say yes to a relationship. I want you to marry me,to be my partner for life." He handed me a letter. "Wait for me. I will come back and marry you. Never lose hope in me, Deepa."

After that day, we never met again. The letter was the only memory I had of him. No photos, no calls,just words on paper that kept my hope alive.

Years passed. I built a successful career as a guitarist and even opened a music institute for aspiring musicians. Many of our college friends asked about Hari, but I had no answers. There was no message, no sign of him. Some days, I thought he had forgotten me, but his last words kept my faith alive.

Every year, on our graduation day, I would return to this beach with his letter, waiting. But for three years, my

wish remained unfulfilled.
One evening, as I stood on the shore, lost in thought, my mother called. "Deepa, there's a new marriage proposal for you. Are you ready now?" I hesitated before replying, "No, Ma." She sighed. "Are you waiting for someone?"

I remained silent and slowly walked away from the beach. Suddenly, a small

child ran up to me, grabbing my hand. "Say yes to me! I'll be with you forever!" Confused, I knelt down. "Who told you that?"
The child pointed to a man standing in the distance, holding a bouquet of roses and a letter. My heart stopped. It was Hari.

He shouted, "Deepa! I wrote you another letter! Thank you for waiting for me. I will never leave you again. I spent these years building our future, making sure we would have a life without struggles. I've started my own business and secured my career. Now, I'm here,to take care of our family, to be with you forever."

Tears welled up in my eyes. I stood frozen. "Who said yes to you? You disappeared for three years without a single message. Why should I believe you now?"

Hari took a deep breath. "You're mistaken, Deepa. I didn't come back to ask you to be in a relationship." I frowned. "Then why are you here?" He smiled. "To propose to you, Deepa. Let's get married."

A sob escaped my lips. Overwhelmed, I ran toward him, throwing my arms around him. "Do I still need to say yes?" Hari chuckled. "No expectations." Their journey of waiting, built on hope, had finally reached its destination. They met their families and had a beautiful arranged marriage.

After years of waiting, Deepa found her revenge in the most hilarious way, making Hari do all the house chores for the rest of his life. He accepted every punishment with a smile because he was the one who had first confessed, first loved, and first dreamed of their future together.

The once-playful flirt had transformed into a devoted husband, proving that no matter how much a man flirts, when he finds the one, he belongs only to her.
Their love endured because of hope, the unwaning moon of desires that never faded, even through years of silence.

Sachin Venkat

Just a common man, who is trying to know who he is!!

ஆண் நொடிகள்

கடிகார நொடி முள்;

நடுத்தர வீட்டின் ஆண்,

நிற்கின்ற நொடி, பாழடைகிறார்.

பணமா? நேரமா?

ஆசை, தேவை மறைத்து மறந்து,

ஏக்கத்தை கூலியாகக் கொண்டு,

மகிழ்ச்சி என்ற சிறு நேரத்திற்கு,

உழைப்பின் வலிகள் போற்றப்படாமலும்,

சுயநலமின்றி ஓடி,

குடும்பக் கடிகாரத்தின் முதல் அடி,

ஆண் நொடிகள்.

A.Beo Bency Salate

My name is Beo Bency, and I'm a lover of words and stories. While I don't consider myself a passionate author, I have a deep affection for writing and the power it holds to connect us, inspire us, and transform us. I'm a passionate author, I've always found joy in the act of writing. There's something therapeutic about putting pen to paper, about watching words flow onto the page, and about crafting stories that transport us to new worlds.I'm grateful for the gift of writing and the joy it brings to my life.

My heart beats with a lonely sigh, Aching for a love that's yet to arrive. A longing that cannot be defined,
A yearning that echoes, heart and mind.

In moonlit nights, I search the sky, Hoping to find a glimpse of you, passing by.
The stars up high, a twinkling sea, A celestial map, guiding me to thee.
Memories of what could be, haunt me still,
A bittersweet reminder, of love's unfulfilled will.
So I'll hold on to hope, and never let go, For in the darkness, a light will glow.

Kadambari Gupta

She has a P.G, LL.B. by qualification and a writer by passion and is a published co-author of over one thousand anthologies.

Longing

I was longing to meet him,
As seen and exchanged greetings on social media,
Thought how will it be to meet and greet,
In person Shake hands, exchange pleasantries, Now this longing has down to never ending, Suffering and misery,
As suffering from acute pain in chest and back,
Admitted to hospital doctors fried to revive his heart couldn't bring him back, The longing unfortunately had an ending so sad has an ending so sad

E. Nikhila

Writing has always been a personal hobby. Much later with muster up courage and support of well-wishers, I began writing openly around the end of 2023.

Heart of a soldier in the realm of ruin
Cries of a child in the middle of chaos for a familiar hand Unspoken confession of a teen towards one-sided love Thoughts of elderly witnessing laughter of youth
Silence of a heart that mourns a loss Eyes of a stray pet for the touch of care
As beautiful as it seems, it is a painful feeling. The art of longing which is beautifully painful...!

Kanupriya Iyer

Kanupriya Iyer is an artist based in Chennai, India. She has published two books, Humsuffers and The Family Lockdown. Her short stories have been published online and, in an anthology, titled The Fiction Collective. A theatre and film enthusiast, she has also written, directed and acted in plays and short films.

YOU COULD ASK ME HOW I DO MY NAILS

You could ask me how I do my nails and I'd smile
(I wish my highs weren't punctuated by nothingness.)

I'd pretend to wave you off and turn away
(To crave, just once, the satisfaction of a job well done.)

The sun could hit my berry hair at just the right angle
(Am I doing too much?)
A purpled you could notice and tell me to pose (Then why does it all feel like so little?)

I wouldn't know what to do with my hands (I ache to be held)
They would tug at each other awkwardly (But I sneer at needing to hold on.)
I could return the favour and hide behind the phone
(Does the oak ever feel like crawling back into the acorn?)
I could keep clicking until you tell me you're done (Why do I feel like I'll never know?)
You could tell me about this new earworm
(If I tire of everything I love, what will I live for?) and call it music for a goldfish
(Maybe if I don't think, I won't feel.)

I could laugh and call it my favourite just to spite you
(Bury myself in work and call it moving on.)

And you could call me crazy and wrap your arms around me I'd still struggle to say yes to happiness.

You could say you want to watch me do my nails next time. And I could smile.

Dr. Nuthi Abhilash

DR. NUTHI ABHILASH, from Telangana, India, is a distinguished educator, poet, and author with over 'nine years 'of experience. His multifaceted career includes roles as an educational mentor, guide, and poet, having written more than 1,500 poems in English, alongside numerous works in Telugu and Hindi. His literary achievements also include over '100 inspirational stories' published in esteemed newspapers.

Dr.Nuthi Abhilash's dedication to education is evidenced by his receipt of two
"WORLD RECORD'S" and two "DOCTORATE'S "(H.C).

His honors include the "TELANGANA RATNA AWARD ", "NATIONAL INSPIRATIONAL MONUMENT AWARD", "NATIONAL NANDI AWARD", "SAHITHI CHANDRA NAME AWARD", and the "NATIONAL PEN

AWARD".and honored with the "Best Talent of the Year Award "in 2023. Additionally, Dr. Abhilash has earned more than "130 national and international" certificates in a range of educational topics.

Moon's Vigil

High above in the silent sky,
A silver eye drifts calm and shy.
It hears my whispers, feels my sighs, A watcher of my sleepless nights.

I send my wishes, soft yet bright, Like fallen stars in quiet flight.
The moon just lingers, still and wise, Holding secrets in its light.
It watches as my heart unfolds, Spilling stories left untold.
A patient witness, vast and deep, Guarding dreams I dare not keep.
Through every phase, through every tide, It stays so close, yet just outside.
A quiet glow, a knowing gleam, The moon that watches over me.

Chenjerai Mhondera

Chenjerai Mhondera is an internationally acclaimed visionary writer, critic, and innovator with over 600 publications across Zimbabwe, South Africa, Kenya, Cameroon, Nigeria, India, USA, Latin America, and Serbia. A winner of over 420 literary awards, who pioneered the HiCoup writing form and critiques conventional language and alphabet. As a dissident reporter, editor, and book reviewer, Chenjerai champions social justice and literary innovation, and is a member of various writers' organizations in Africa, India, Pakistan and the world beyond.

A place to hide joy

I am looking for a place to hide my happiness Because elsewhere it's not free from harm, The hater pursuing its life with hatred intense, And the pretender wanting it never to live, Flourish and be a blessing lived
Maybe this place is you!
Keep it safe, and in it you shall be sorrow never again!

V Hrishikesh

An Engineering graduate who's into writing stories. Mostly into writing longer stories and here I'm trying my best with shorter

Unopened

The wine bottle sat forgotten in the corner of her kitchen cabinet, coated in a thin layer of dust. She stared at it, unsure whether to laugh or cry. She remembered the night it appeared, four years ago, the night she thought he was going to propose. Instead, he handed her the bottle with a nervous smile and said, "We'll open this together." Then he vanished. No texts. No calls. Just... gone.

There was no single clue about him. She was devastated. She started to replay everything in her head again and again, did she misread the vibe? Was it just a fling? Or did he just get bored? Had she imagined the love between them? Or was he just full of lies?

She tried to move on, at least she thought she did. She dated many people, but no one seemed to fill the emptiness he left behind. Each relationship felt hollow, like she was forcing herself to forget him by replacing him. It didn't work.

"How are you going to justify this?" she asked in a text she never sent. Across the city, he sat alone in his dimly lit apartment, scrolling through old photos on his phone. He told himself he wouldn't do this anymore, yet here he was, staring at her smile, frozen in time. The smile that once made him feel safe, now left him haunted.

He had loved her deeply. But love wasn't enough. He remembered her tantrums, the way she dismissed his feelings, the endless accusations. He remembered the night she called him a pervert, the words ringing in his head like a siren. He tried to convince her it was a mistake, that he wasn't trying to hurt her, but she refused to believe him. After that, something inside him broke. He kept trying, for months, swallowing his feelings, apologizing for things that weren't his fault, convincing himself she would change. But she didn't. Every conversation became an exhausting cycle of blame and guilt. She never remembered the quiet moments when he stayed up late to calm her down after a panic attack. She forgot the nights he sacrificed sleep to help her with assignments or the times he patiently listened when she spiralled into self- doubt. All she remembered were his mistakes, the moments where he wasn't perfect.

He loved her, but he couldn't keep losing himself to her insecurities. So, he walked away.

For her, his disappearance felt like abandonment. She thought about every fight, how she lashed out when he was busy, how she accused him of neglect whenever he didn't respond fast enough. She never considered that maybe he was hurting too, that maybe his silence wasn't indifference, but exhaustion. She never realized he had been holding everything inside until he couldn't anymore.

Now, staring at that unopened bottle, she wondered what they could've been if she had just listened, if she had met his patience with understanding instead of anger. She wondered if he had loved her enough to stay if she had just loved him the way he needed, quietly, patiently, without judgment.

Meanwhile, he sat on his apartment floor, wondering if she had ever truly seen him, if she ever knew how much he was carrying alone. He had spent his whole life hiding his feelings to be strong for others, and for once, he thought he had found someone with whom he could be vulnerable. But instead, he felt misunderstood, accused, and drained.

Both of them longed for each other, her, for the comfort she once felt . him, for the person he once believed she could become. Yet neither reached out. The silence felt safer than risking more heartbreak.

The unopened bottle sat in her kitchen. The dusty screen of his phone glowed with her photo. Neither one knew that they were both still waiting, waiting for the courage to face the past, or for time to finally dull the ache of what could've been.

Dr. Hemalatha V

I'm Dr. Hemalatha V, Assistant Professor (Senior Grade) in the Department of English at Saveetha Engineering College, with 17 years of teaching experience. I completed my B.A. and M.A. in English Literature from Quaid–E-Millath Government College for Women, followed by an M.Phil from the University of Madras and a Ph.D. in American Literature in 2023.
Over the years, I've published 7 research papers in Scopus and UGC CARE- listed journals, co-authored 2 books, and filed 2 patents. I've presented my work at several national and international conferences, focusing on English Language Teaching and Indian Writing in

English. I'm also a certified Cambridge Business English (Vantage) professional and an active member of ELTAI.

My Prolonged Longing

My longing for self-respect in our nation endures,
Whenever I see beggars crowding public places,
Whenever I see politicians posing with pretension,
Whenever I see officials tangled in corruption,
I long for a time when the world aligns with mine! My
longing for self-discipline persists,
When I watch our youth intoxicating themselves with
drugs, When I watch graduates engaging in illegal acts,
When the news reports of molestation and gang rape, I
long for a time when the world aligns with mine!
My longing for patriotic citizens remains, When the
educated spoil public property, When drivers ignore the
rules,
When our rivers are choked with litter,
I long for a time when the world aligns with mine! My
longing for self -identity grows,
When adults forsake identity for fleeting modernity,
When criminals thrive under cyber anonymity, When
children waste time on video games,
I long for a time when the world aligns with mine! I
yearn to see clean water reservoirs,
I yearn to see people sharing real love and happiness,
I yearn to see selfless leaders who truly serve our nation,
I hope for a time when the world harmonizes with mine!

Shaikh hamd

I am a high school student interested in history, geography, and science. I find history and geography so interesting because they unveil the stories of other cultures and how people and places have influenced the world. I find science interesting because it has the capability to explain phenomena naturally occurring in the environment and address problems faced in the real world. My interest in science stemmed from personal experiences, particularly in fields such as health and technology. Aspects to love about science include linking in with history and geography that offer a unique way to understand the world. Besides, writing is one among other hobbies that I enjoy for creating fiction that inspires, entertained, or non-fiction depicting or reflecting on real events of issues experienced; through writing, I convey an idea and connect my various interests in creative ways by reading and learning how this passion intersects in my extra time. I am expecting to fuse my knowledge with my creativity toward making a difference in life.

The Unwaning Moon of Desires

The moon suspended in the dark sky, shining and unwaning, just as the desires that had planted themselves in Ayaan's heart. He had always thought that love was ephemeral, a transient breeze that whispered through one's existence before disappearing into the abyss. But then there was Zoya,his yearning, his poetry, his moon.
They had agreed to meet at the old library by the derelict clock tower, where

dust swirled in the golden beams of sunlight streaming through the windows. Ayaan was immersed in the couplets of Ghalib, his fingers following the fine ink of ancient Urdu couplets, when a gentle voice broke his isolation.

"Do you always read poetry by yourself?"
He glanced up, and there she was,Zoya. She was like the smell of rain on dry land, surprising yet calming. From the time that day, they read together, argued about Mir and Faiz, and filled the studious library with laughter and sneaked glances.

But destiny had other plans.
Zoya was engaged to a man she had never seen. Ayaan was aware of this, but each moment spent with her made his heart grow heavier with longing. Each night, he witnessed her walk away as the sun set, casting long shadows of potential love upon the ground.

One evening, as they sat under the moonlight, Ayaan

whispered, "Can love be without fulfillment, Zoya?"
She smiled, her eyes reflecting the same agony he felt. “Perhaps love is not meant to be fulfilled, Ayaan. Perhaps it lives in longing, in the spaces between what is and what could be.”

The wedding arrived like a storm, swift and inevitable. Ayaan stood at a distance, watching the woman he loved disappear into a life where he could not follow.

Years went by, but the library stayed. Ayaan continued to read poetry by himself, but he never really was. The pages bore her voice, the ink contained her laughter, and the moon above did not change,unwaning, as was his longing for a love that was never his to begin with.

Because some loves are not destined to be inscribed into existence; they are destined to be found in verses, in yearning, in the soft pain of an unending moon.

Jaya Sree P

Jaya Sree P is an engineering student with a passion for writing and exploration. At just 16, she began her journey as a junior journalist for Chutti Vikatan, a leading magazine, honing her storytelling and investigative skills. Beyond academics, she is an avid reader and passionate traveler, always seeking new experiences and perspectives. Her diverse interests blend technical knowledge with creativity, making her writing both insightful and engaging.

The Home I Carry

Vahimathi sat by the window of her small apartment, watching the rain trickle down the glass. The city was alive outside, horns blaring, people rushing, neon lights reflecting on the wet pavement. But her mind was somewhere else, somewhere far away.
It had been ten years since she had left her hometown. She had shifted more than five places, but her heart had been stuck with the greasy smell of her old water motor in her hometown.

Her muddy charcoal wood water stove heater had been stuck in her eyes. The charcoal color had never faded from her hands.

The kitchen chimney with her mom's lovely smile

Her Grandma's cheeky smile when she supports my mischief from mom My mini cycle that had a falling chain over and over
Cute Barbie dolls all over my bedroom Those cute abcd magnets in cupboard Still a 1000 of things has been left there
Life moved fast after they left, school, college, each milestone pulling her further from the home she had once known. But no matter how much she tried to build a new life, there was an ache deep within her, a longing that refused to fade.
Every road she walked had always reminded her of the roads around her home. She always dreamt of going there. But was it always going to be just a dream… or ?

M. Cherina Mary

A weaver of words and a seeker of untold emotions, the co-author finds solace in the rhythm of storytelling. With ink-stained dreams and a heart attuned to the echoes of human longing, they write to unravel the delicate dance between love, loss and healing. Each story is a whisper of the soul, a bridge between past wounds and future hope. In the quiet corners of life, where emotions stir like the wind, they listen, they feel and they write, so that no one feels alone in their journey.

Echoes of Longing

The city lights flickered beyond the rain-smeared window, casting fleeting shadows across the walls. Racheal traced the outline of her reflection, the storm outside mirroring the one within her. She had grown now, but the ache remained a relentless longing that refused to loosen its grip.

She remembered the small, cluttered living room where laughter once filled the air. Her father, Alex, had been her anchor, his presence a constant reassurance. But one night, the echoes of a single fight shattered that warmth. Harsh words, followed by unbearable silence, turned the house into a hollow space. Alex withdrew behind the weight of his own regrets and though he stayed, Racheal felt abandoned.

Years passed. She built a life of independence, a careful facade of strength. People admired her resilience, praised her determination. But no applause could quiet the emptiness. Beneath her accomplishments, she was still the little girl who longed for her father's embrace.

Then came Robin.

He was light, laughing, patient and steady. His love softened the walls she'd built. With Robin, Racheal caught glimpses of the warmth she had once known. But love, to her, was a fragile thing. She waited for it to break. Every smile from Robin was shadowed by fear. Every tender moment felt like a prelude to loss.

The longing twisted her thoughts. She pushed him away, testing the strength of his affection. When he stayed, it unsettled her. How could love endure without fracture?

She saw echoes of her father's withdrawal in the most innocent of silences.
Then came the night that broke her. A trivial argument spiraled into accusations. Robin's patience wavered and for the first time, he walked away. The storm outside raged as Racheal stood frozen, the empty silence pressing against her chest. Her phone lay on the table, the screen glowing with unanswered calls. The choice hung before her, heavy and trembling.
In one world, her trembling hands reached for the phone. She called Robin, her voice cracking with regret. She spoke of the fears she could no longer hide, the walls she had built. Robin listened. His forgiveness didn't erase the past, but it offered a future. Slowly, she reached out to her father too and though the pain lingered, healing began. Each step was uncertain, but the longing in her heart found solace.
In another world, she turned away. The phone's glow dimmed. She convinced herself she was better off alone. Days turned into weeks, the ache within her dulled but never disappeared. She avoided places where laughter echoed, where lovers walked hand in hand. The walls she built stood firm, shielding her from the risk of heartbreak, but also from love.
Two choices. Two fates!

But the longing remained.
Note: Childhood trauma shapes us, influencing how we love and heal. While we can't change the past, we can choose to confront our pain and seek support. Healing is possible and you don't have to face it alone.

Rekha

A lackadaisical student, a compulsive day-dreamer, an aspiring poet by passion. Weaving words into emotions, articulating fleeting moments in verses. Writing started as a spur of the moment passion, which soon became an introspective reflection. Now trying my best for my first anthology as a co author.

Lost in the Haze

Moments we once held dear to our hearts, I wonder where they are now?
All the complacent smiles with no worries, I wonder if we can smile like that again? Days with unforeseeable surprises,
Is there anything now worth being surprised about? Those foolishly grandeur promises we made,
Do we even have the courage to recollect them now? That adrenaline rush of trying new things,
Do we no longer take up a challenge?
That simple-minded happiness we fundamentally had, Do we now need a big reason to be happy?
That competitive spirit that drove us to the edge, Did we lose the spirit of warrior in us?
That ever-consuming passion of ours, Did we really ruthlessly extinguish it?
That fragile heart which ingratiatingly seeks for expression, Did we lock it in an inaccessible corner?
Those wings of freedom we carried on our back, Did we willingly put ourselves in a prison?
That over-the-top positivity we carried as an armour, Did we lose it in a tough battle?
That happy-go lucky personality of ours,
Did we fall victim to our own circumstances?
These never-ending self-doubts, these ever-problematic fears, this unrealistic longing for respite.
Much needed respite is unlocked only when you let your highly sophisticated brain to stop producing never-happening scary movies?
This longing for my brain to become my best friend is

the one and only longing I wish to overcome.

Bhargava S

My poetry explores the intricate relationship between pain and beauty, finding artistic expression in the human experience of suffering. I work part- time, crafting verses that attempt to capture the raw emotional landscape of life. My mother, who has passed, remains a profound source of inspiration and love, deeply influencing my perspective and creative work.

Deafen by the thoughts

As the echoes of the past blaring through my ears,
the grand moment of tragedy was lost along with the cause the only remains are broken truth,
hearts and time that doesn't pause,
tears have dried so they can't bring back time when they sleep. maybe they took the agony with them and evaporated
I am trying hard to weep I am trying hard to weep

Meenadshi

Software Enthusiast | Content Creator | Poet

He too existed - only as a poem…

I didn't know your name until it found its way into my unwritten verses. You were never close, not in hallways, not in classes,
just a silhouette carved
into the backdrop of my becoming.
You appeared in fragments,
a glimpse by the library stairs, a half-smile at a fest
that left echoes in my chest for days.
We never met. Not really.
But I knew the way your voice dipped at the end of a laugh, and how your presence turned the ordinary,
into something almost cinematic.

I remembered you
in the scent of cold evenings, in the hush of late-night walks where even the moon felt
like it was keeping your secret.

I never wanted you to know. Because some desires bloom in the shadow of silence, and you,
you were the poem
I never meant to write but couldn't stop living.

Pooja Kharade

I'm Pooja, a writer & creative soul with a passion for storytelling & self-expression. Through @mysoulwrites16, I share my thoughts, emotions & experiences, hoping to inspire & connect with like-minded in

MONARCH OF THE NIGHT

Sky inhabited with stary light,
Peeping through the window
at the sparkling moon is a heartful delight, Dreaming limitlessly with no height
To attain them, be a wright let the wings of our notions get an another flight,
Triumphing over every affliction like a knight Being an anxious, despite
Drowse and let the calmness unite After all the strains,
a new day will always be risen alright Let's begin each day merrily
by smiling more than a little bright !

Sambit Mishra

Sambit Mishra is a writer and poet whose work explores the emotional terrains of longing, memory, and human desire. With a voice both lyrical and introspective, his writing has appeared in various literary spaces, resonating with readers who seek depth and quiet truth. When not writing, he delves into philosophy and nature, drawing inspiration from silence, shadows, and the unspoken corners of the soul.

The Hollow Echo of Want

There is a kind of hunger that no feast can sate. It clings to the ribs like a remembered name or a half-sung melody, something once close enough to touch but never held long enough to claim. This is longing,not a fire, but a slow, cold ache. A winter housed in the soul.
We do not often speak of yearning in the daylight. It wears no perfume, it doesn't ask politely. It enters uninvited through dreams, through scents that brush past on city streets, through old photographs half-faded and tucked away behind newer joys. Desire, in its rawest form, is not about what we can have, but what we *almost* had,or never dared reach for at all.

The ancient poets, those who built verses with trembling hands, understood this well. They whispered to distant lovers, to gods who never replied, to lives that could have been theirs in some kinder version of the world. They penned sonnets not for consummation, but for the delicious ache of absence. They fed their yearning to the moon, that unwaning witness to all our nightbound cravings.

And the moon listened. It always does.

Longing lives between what is and what could be. It's the glance held a moment too long. The letter never sent. The home one never returns to, but dreams of incessantly. It sharpens the senses. It writes its name on the inside of our eyelids, so we see it every time we close our eyes.

But make no mistake,yearning is not weakness. It is not the frailty of hearts too soft. No, it is the strength to keep reaching toward something that may never reach back. It is the belief that somewhere beyond the known, there is a better echo waiting. It is love that dares remain unfulfilled, because in the ache, we remain alive.

We are all pilgrims of desire. And some of us walk not to arrive, but to remember why we began the journey.
So let the moon rise again. Let it shine on the letters never sent, the songs never sung, the hands never held.
Let it illuminate the gentle, persistent truth:
That to yearn is to be human. And to long is to hope.
And hope, even unreturned, is a light that never dies.

Sarah cope

Sarah is a novice writer of child and adult fiction and a published poet. Writing became Sarah's saviour, after surviving a domestic violence relationship, then being diagnosed with a chronic illness, dyslexia (I know right a writer with dyslexic really?), and then the cherry on top ADHD. Luckily, she's had a great support network who have convinced Sarah to continue to write, despite all the obstacles she has faced and is still facing. So Sarah continues to believe and follow that dream.

I wonder what's on cloud nine

I wonder what its like up on cloud nine, Would the weather up there be fine, Would the storm in my head clear,
Would it free me of all my anxiety and fear,

I wonder what it would be like up on cloud nine, Would it just cross over country borderlines, Or would it take me up into the sky,
Would it take me to a city in clouds up high

A city ive only ever imagine in your minds eye, A place of peace a place where life is beautified
That's free of impurities and the evils of our world,
A place I could only dream of, I guess it is a Dreamworld,
Oh how I wonder what it would be like on cloud nine
Would the weather up there be fine,
Would the storm in my head clear,
Would it free me of all my anxiety and fear,

Stoic Vin

About: Stoic Vin is a poet and writer who finds inspiration in life's quiet truths, fleeting emotions, and the unspoken depth of human connections.

His writings often reflect themes of love, loss, healing, and self-discovery. For him, writing is not just a passion but a journey—a way to capture moments, embrace honesty, and connect with souls beyond boundaries.

I Still Remember

I still remember that moment— You walked away,
The words caught in my throat,
And how you vanished into a sea of faces.
I remember the moments we shared, The quiet steps to the temple,
The way your voice felt like a melody,
And our first meeting, as if written in the stars.
I remember the way your smile lit the world, How my gaze lingered,
The gift you gave that I still treasure,
And the fear that held my heart from speaking.
I remember every word you spoke,
How time paused the moment you arrived, Our last conversation echoed in my mind, And my last night in your city—
A memory I carry is like a fading photograph. And yet, with every memory, a quiet ache remains.
Did you remember me, too?
~ Stoic Vin

A.M. Adeline Jane

About: A.M Adeline Jane is a 6th grader studying at Velammal Vidhyashram, Surapet having a great passion for writing stories and poems. She has won The first prize in St.Anthony's Church, Symphony of singers singing competition in Nov 2025

The Lonely Woman

Once there lived a very lonely old woman. She lives in a small broken house but every evening a teenager named Martha came and visited her every day. As soon as she was about to leave. The elderly woman would give her a cup cake, this became a routine.

It has been almost 12 years and Martha left the town for a job, but the woman didn't know the situation. The old woman, unaware of her departure, continued waiting, watching the moon wondering 'Where is Martha? She usually visits me, now what happened?' She asked everyone but everyone said 'NO'. The elderly woman was helpless.

One day she felt very dizzy. She went to the doctor; the doctor sadly told the woman that she only had one day left to live. She went home sadly. After a day, it was her birthday and Martha came back, she is now successful and bought many gifts for the woman. She witnessed something unexpected.

While driving to her house there was a terrible thunderstorm, the car was stopped by a crazy woman, the woman said "You Shall Not Pass!" After many arguments, the woman finally let them go. They continued their way. On the way, Martha had an important shooting, she was ready but before the shooting she saw a copy of herself as a mannequin but weirder. She got confused. She went to the photographer and said "What is she doing here?" She realized that it was almost midnight. She completed the shooting and quickly went back to the car.

That very night, Martha returned, now a successful

woman, her arms full of gifts. She hurried to the old house, only to find a single cupcake and a letter resting on the table. Trembling, she read the words: My dear Martha, you have always been my brightest star. If you ever wonder where to find me, just look at the moon—my desires never waned, just like its light. But out of no where the woman jumped out and popped millions of balloons. Martha screamed at the top of her lungs. Turns out, the woman death was a prank. She celebrated her birthday with her best friend Martha. She gave the elderly woman the biggest hug. She took the cupcake and gone back to her own house. Since then, Martha came to the elderly woman's house to brighten up her day.

Miriam Sam

About: Educational Qualification - Btech in Electronics and Communication Engineering, MBA in Operations and Marketing

Yet to conquer my heart's desire

Still awaiting to make my dream come true, May be one
day, I will achieve it,
May be not
But I do not wish to be hopeless, My life has not ended,
So, the opportunities are endless before me

www.ingramcontent.com/pod-product-compliance
Ingram Content Group UK Ltd.
Pitfield, Milton Keynes, MK11 3LW, UK
UKHW021410190726
13845UKWH00028B/991

9 788199 785670